Laurie Tells

by Linda Lowery
illustrations by John Eric Karpinski

 Carolrhoda Books, Inc./Minneapolis

I extend my gratitude and warm wishes to the members of the Children's Court Advisory Board of Walworth County, Wisconsin. Special thanks to the following people who have been so dedicated in speaking out on behalf of the children: Judge Robert Kennedy, Judge James Carlson, Judge John Race, Reverend Sue D'Alessio, Richard Peterson, District Attorney Phillip Koss, Victim/Witness Coordinator Mary Koss, Dr. Bonni Van Gorder, Human Services Investigator Theresa Hanson, Linda Abel, Bonnie Hocker, and Wisconsin State Representative Chuck Coleman. Also many thanks to Jill Anderson, my editor, for her sensitive questions and perceptive suggestions.

—L.L.

Special thanks to Shari Tretow for serving as my model—and my inspiration—for Laurie. Thanks also to my parents, Jean and John, for their steadfastness; my brother David and my sister Beverly; the kind-hearted nurturing of Dan and Jennifer Gerhartz; Carole Pomeday, for her acuteness; Barbara Peterson, who challenges me; Lisa Edelblute, who heals by listening; and to the Rev. Robert C. Zick and Marian Eshrich for responding to my appeal. I thank God for seeing this day.

—J.E.K.

This book is available in two editions:
Library binding by Carolrhoda Books, Inc.
Soft cover by First Avenue Editions
c/o The Lerner Group
241 First Avenue North
Minneapolis, Minnesota 55401

LIBRARY OF CONGRESS CATALOGING-IN-PUBLICATION DATA

Lowery, Linda.
   Laurie Tells / by Linda Lowery ; illustrations by John Eric Karpinski.
     p. cm.
   Summary: When her mother doesn't believe her, eleven-year-old Laurie tells a supportive aunt that she is being sexually abused by her father.
   ISBN 0-87614-790-2 (lib. bdg.)
   ISBN 0-87614-961-1 (pbk.)
   [1. Child molesting—Fiction. 2. Incest—Fiction. 3. Fathers and daughters—Fiction.]
I. Karpinski, John Eric, ill. II. Title.
PZ7.L9653Lau 1994
[Fic]—dc20
                                                     93-9786
                                                     CIP
                                                      AC

Manufactured in the United States of America

2 3 4 5 6 7 – P/JR – 00 99 98 97 96 95

For my sisters,
with love
—L.L.

For Dan Comeau
—J.E.K.

"I'm going for a walk," I tell my mother.
"I'll be back soon."
But I wish I were never coming back.
I wish I could walk to Australia, to China,
and never have to see his face again.

"Be back in time for supper," my mother says.
"I will," I say.
I don't look at her.
On days like this, I can't look at anyone.
I can't even look in the mirror.
My feet step out onto the porch.
They take me down the stairs.

Outside, the leaves whirl around in cyclones.
I walk along the curb
where he and I used to burn leaves together.
Every fall, we would rake leaves into piles
and light a huge fire.
The flames licked at the sky like dragon's breath.
I would back away, scared that monsters and spooks
might jump out and get me at any minute.

But now it's not the monsters and spooks
that scare me.
Now it's my dad.

———

I walk down the street,
my insides as empty as the trees
that have lost their leaves.
Paper and dust swirl in the wind
around me.
The grit scratches my eyes.

I'm so cold.
Even if I stood right in the middle of a fire,
I'd stay cold to my bones.
Still, I don't bother to close my jacket.
It doesn't matter.
Nothing matters.

It's hard to believe
how happy I used to be,
strolling down this same street
on my way to the beach.
I loved how my feet tingled
on the warm pavement.
I loved how tan and warm my body was.
I don't know if my body will ever
feel that good again.
I have places on my body
I don't want anyone to touch.
They're mine, only for me,
and it makes me sick
to think he touched me there.

The first time it happened,
I was nine.
He was saying good-night,
scratching my back.
And then he reached
under my nightgown
and touched my body all over.
He pressed his heavy body
against mine.
I hated what he was doing to me.
I began to cry.
Even when I cried,
he kept leaning, pressing, touching.
My nightgown got all rumpled up
around my neck.
And he still didn't stop.
Why didn't he stop?

———

The wind slaps my scarf across my cheek, hard.
Sometimes I wish
I'd been born in Brazil, in the hot jungle.
Or in Tahiti. Or in Africa.
Mostly, I wish I were someone else's daughter.

Could my dad really have loved me the way I remember?
One winter I got lost
coming home from kindergarten.
All the houses looked so big and strange,
I wandered far away looking for mine.
Block after block went by,
house after strange house,
until finally I sat down on a snowhill,
knowing I'd never find my way home again.
But suddenly there he was,
jumping from the car,
running to sit down beside me.
He'd been looking for me for an hour.
He put his arm around me,
and I snuggled up against him, safe.
I wish I could always be
as happy as I was then,
sitting on that snowhill with my dad.
Just him and me,
forever.

But now things are different—
his eyes, his laugh.
The same hands that pushed me on the park swings,
the same hands that buttoned me into my coat,
now are too big, too touchy, everywhere.

———

Whack!
I kick a stone so hard it ricochets off a hubcap
and comes back at me, flying.
My secret is eating away
a dark, hollow pit inside me.
Every time we're alone,
I wonder
if he will touch me that way again.
The hole in my gut
keeps getting deeper,
emptier.
I can't hide this anymore.
I have to tell.

Once, I did try to tell—
last year, when I was ten.
My dad was gone, working late,
and my mother was in the kitchen.
"Something bad is happening in our family,"
I told my mother.
"I think I should tell you about it."
She stopped doing the dishes
and turned and looked at me.
"What is it?" she asked.
"It's Dad," I said.
"Sometimes when he comes in to say good-night,
he . . . touches me."
I was looking down,
twisting the noodles on my plate
around, around my fork.
"Of course he touches you," she said.
"He gives you back-rubs."
"No, Mom," I said.

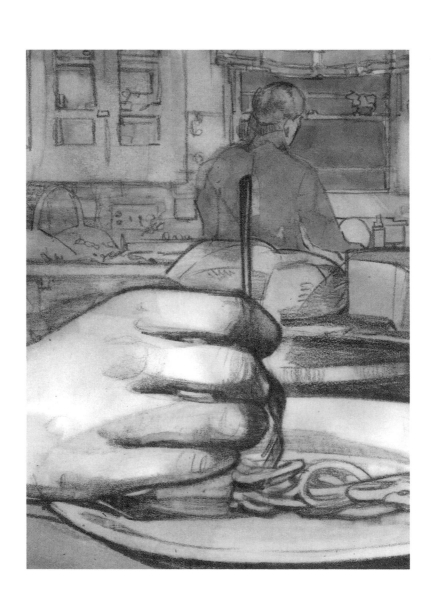

How could I tell her
the places he touched me?
It made my stomach sick
to think of saying it out loud.
"He touches me . . .
under my nightgown.
He leans against me.
I don't like it."
My mother gave me a strange look,
like when I came home from first grade
and told her my teacher had pointy teeth
and that I was afraid he was a monster.

"I think you're imagining things,"
said my mother.
"Your dad would never, ever
do a thing like that.
He loves you."
"But, Mom . . ." I started to say.
"If you don't want him
to rub your back anymore,
tell him," she said.
"And don't get carried away by your imagination."
She turned back to the dishes in the sink.
"Go and do your homework," she said then.
Her voice sounded very flat,
like we were finished talking.

———

I am by the lake now,
far from home.
I can picture my mother's back that day
as if she were still standing
right in front of me.
She didn't believe me.
If my own mother won't believe me,
who will?
Who will listen?

Crumpled leaves float on the cold, gray water.
A gull screams overhead.
I want to scream too:
"Why? Why is he hurting me like this?"
I want to fly away,
never to come back again,
ever.

I sit down on a rock,
my back to the wind.
I wrap my arms around my knees
and curl up
like a caterpillar that rolls itself into a ball
to protect its soft insides from harm.

My insides are soft too,
and they hurt so much.
If you could see feelings,
mine would be all raw and red.
At least if I had a broken arm,
everyone would notice it.
But my pain is hidden.
I don't know anyone I can show my feelings to.

I watch the leaves toss
in the waves of the lake.
They look like the faces of people I know.
My grandmother floats by,
and I think of our Saturday afternoon card games.
We have fun,
but we never talk about serious things.
Besides, her face reminds me of my mother's—
my mother who didn't believe me.
No, I can't tell my grandmother.

Another leaf looks like my next-door neighbor.
He always waves when I leave for school.
He likes me.
But he likes my father too.
They talk and laugh over the fence
all the time.
No, I don't think I can trust him with my secret.

Now my music teacher floats by,
with her kind eyes and her kind smile.
She's my favorite.
But she's too nice and happy
to ever believe something this terrible.
She might not even know what I'm talking about.

A bright yellow leaf flutters down among
the brown ones.
I think of my aunt Jan
and how she looks me straight in the eye
when we talk,
as if I'm a grown-up.
She doesn't do everything my dad says.
She doesn't laugh loud at his jokes,
the way some people do.
My aunt might listen to me.
She might even believe me.

I bury my head in my knees.
What if she tells my father?
Then what?
Will he make fun of me?
Call me a liar?
Will he hurt me?

My aunt has never been afraid of my dad,
even when they were kids.
Something tells me
she'll know what to do.
Something tells me
she won't let him hurt me again.

———

I hardly remember getting to the gas station,
to the phone.
I search for a coin in my pocket,
put in the money, and dial the number.
The wind whips around me.

"Hello?"
Aunt Jan's voice sounds cheerful, familiar.
I swallow hard. I clear my throat.
My fingers play with the sign on the phone.
"It's Laurie," I say. "May I come over?"
Her house is two miles from here,
but it doesn't feel far.
Today I'd walk twenty miles to find Aunt Jan.
Maybe two hundred.
"Is something wrong?" she asks.
"Y-yes . . . N-no . . . Y-yes," I say.
"I'll come and pick you up," she offers.
"But I'm not at home."
"Just tell me where you are, Sweetie," she says.
"I'll be right there."
I like how she calls me Sweetie
even though I'm not little anymore.
I like how she doesn't ask me
to explain what's wrong
on the phone.

———

She comes,
and we drive past the park
where Dad used to take me.
I would put my little hand in his big hand,
and we would walk up the hill
to the swings.
He would push me to the clouds,
to the sky.
It was fun, but scary too.
"STOP, DADDY!" I would shout, laughing.

Last night when he came into my room,
I wanted to shout it again:
"STOP, DADDY!"
But nothing came out.
No words.
No screams.

I should have done something
to make him stop.
I shouldn't have been so quiet.
Maybe he thinks I don't mind
being touched that way.
Why was my voice stuck?
Why couldn't I tell him no?

Aunt Jan takes me to her house,
and I watch her heat up the cocoa.
Everything in her kitchen is bright and open,
except me.
I just sit here, tongue-tied.
I'm afraid she'll think I made it up.
I'm afraid she'll think I'm lying.
She sets down the cocoa spoon
and pulls up a chair beside me.
She puts her warm hands around my cold ones.
"Listen," she says, "I can tell something's wrong.
Do you want to talk about it?"

I remember when I was eight,
I told her another secret:
that I wanted to be a ballerina someday,
beautiful and famous,
and she didn't laugh at all.
Instead, she bought season tickets to the ballet,
and that year we saw fourteen dance companies.
Before each performance,
I'd sit in this kitchen
while she wrapped my hair into a dancer's bun,
just the way I wanted it.
What a nice secret that was,
so different from this one.

I pull my hands away
and stand up.
I have to get this out.
In my head,
I've practiced saying it a million times,
at school and in my dreams
and lying in bed at night after he hurts me.
But now I don't know how to start.
My hands are rubbing together,
sweaty, fast.
I push them through my hair
and stare down at the table.

"It's about Dad and me," I say.
Quickly I look at Aunt Jan,
and I see that it's all right,
that she wants to hear.
"Sometimes he touches me," I say. "My body."
My hands are moving from my mouth to my eyes,
hiding me.
"He's done it lots of times before,
and last night he did it again.
I just want him to stop."

Suddenly
sobs erupt from my stomach.
They rise up through my body
and spill out of my mouth.
"I hate it!" I shout.
Something has broken open inside me now,
and I can't shove it back down.
"I hate what he does to me!"

I hear Aunt Jan cry out
as if she is hurting too.
She is up from her chair,
rushing over to me,
saying something I can't hear.
I only hear my own voice,
echoing loud in my ears.
"I never want to see him again!" I scream.
She reaches to hug me.
I back away, far away,
against the counter.
I don't want anyone to touch me.

Finally I hear my aunt's voice,
warm and urgent.
"How has he hurt you?" she asks.
"Tell me, Laurie. I need to know."
Her eyes are angry.
Is she angry at me?
She pulls a napkin from its ring
and hands it to me gently.
No, she's angry at what I'm telling her.
I reach for the napkin and wipe my tears.
I don't know how she can understand
this terrible thing I'm telling her,
but I see that she wants to.

———

I tell her about last night, in the dark.
I tell her about the other times,
and how I sat in school the next day,
staring out at the tangled mulberry branches
with their dark red stains.
I got all the answers wrong
because I couldn't concentrate on anything.
I could only hope that no one suspected
what had happened to me.

I tell her how maybe it's my fault:
I didn't yell when I should have.
I wonder if people will think I'm a horrible person
because of what has happened.
"Absolutely not," my aunt says.
"You are not to blame. Not even a little."

I tell her how scared I am.
What if he finds out I've told?
I push the napkin hard against my eyes.
"What if after this," I ask,
"Mom and Dad don't want me around anymore?"
"Honey," says my aunt,
"all of us who love you will keep on loving you,
and we will be here with you,
no matter what happens,
no matter how difficult this may be."
I want to believe every word she says.
"It never should have happened in the first place,
and I promise you it won't ever happen again."
She looks straight at me, and I know she means it.

I move toward her, reaching.
It feels good to know she understands.
It feels good to know she believes me.
She takes me in her arms.
I bury my face in her shoulder,
and everything goes blurry.
I can't think. I can't talk.
A soft place opens inside me,
and I just cry and cry
for a long, long time.

———

After a while
I run out of tears,
and I feel light and hungry.
We sit down for our cocoa
and a little supper.
We talk about the summer I stayed with her,
the summer we planted sunflowers.
I want to stay again, now, tonight.
I want to dream about all the happy times
I've had with Aunt Jan.

My aunt tucks me in
under the soft down quilt in her guest room.
She sits on the edge of the bed.
"Do you remember the time we found that owl
with the broken wing,
and we weren't sure what to do?" she asks.
I nod.
I remember how we brought the owl inside
and called lots of people
until we found someone
who would take good care of it
until it could fly again.

"I feel now the way I did then," says my aunt.
"I don't know much about this kind of thing,
and I'm not sure if you can even stay here overnight,
but I have a hunch somebody someplace
will know just what to do."
She brushes a strand of my hair back from my face.
"First I'm going to call your mom
and tell her where you are.
Then—even if it takes all night—
I'll find the right person to help us."

After she goes,
I snuggle deeper into the bed.
I lie there, listening for danger,
like the caterpillar who makes sure it's safe
before uncurling.
The wind howls outside
while my aunt talks quietly on the phone.
I don't move.
I just breathe and listen.
Soon the night gives me its message:
there is nothing hurtful here
in this dark room.
But there is a little jitter inside my heart,
something jumpy.

Just then Aunt Jan comes in and kisses me.
"Can I stay?" I ask.
"Yes," she says. "You can stay."
Instantly I feel
exhausted,
relieved,
as if I could sleep for a hundred years.
I stretch my legs out
as far as they will go beneath the quilt.
I wiggle my toes against the feathers
and sink in deep.
"Good," I say.
Before I can speak another word,
I feel myself drifting off into a bright dream.
My quilt is a silky soft cocoon,
and I am safe and warm
with my aunt beside me.

Author's Note

Not all stories of sexual abuse are like Laurie's. Fathers aren't the only people who abuse children, and mothers often believe and protect their children. Most fathers and mothers hug and kiss and hold their children without ever thinking of touching them in secret or uncomfortable ways.

However, child abuse does happen. And when it does, there is only one way to stop it: by telling the truth. If you are being abused, remember, you are not to blame. The adult who abuses you is. You must get help so that the hurting will stop.

First of all, find someone safe to tell. It might be a teacher or a friend's mother, a neighbor or a doctor, a parent or grandparent, or an aunt or uncle. You will know who is safe to tell by the way you feel about telling that person. If your gut says, "This is not a safe person to tell," you are right! Find another person you feel right about telling.

If you tell someone who does not believe you, or if they ask you to keep it a secret, tell someone else as soon as you can. You might have to tell a few people before you find someone who is strong enough to listen and to believe the truth. Once you tell, there will be a lot of work and a lot of people involved to make sure things get better for you and your family. It will not be easy, but it will be worth it.

It takes a lot of courage to stop abuse. Like Laurie, you CAN find someone who will help you. Abuse can be stopped. Tell someone.